OSCAR

seeks a friend

My thanks to Gérard Moncomble for his help
with the idea for this story. P.P.

LANTANA PUBLISHING

Paweł Pawlak

OSCAR

seeks a friend

Translated by
Antonia Lloyd-Jones

I lost a tooth.

Never mind, I hear you say. But in my case it was a very serious matter. It's hard for a small, ugly skeleton to make friends. And with a tooth missing, I looked so dreadful that I thought I'd never, ever have anyone to play with except Tag.

So one day, when I saw a little girl
burying a tooth in the ground,
I stopped dead.

"Ahem," I coughed, so I wouldn't give her a fright. I asked if she could kindly give me her tooth, to make me look less scary. But all she said was that she needed it too, because if you bury a tooth, your dreams will come true.

Then she looked at me properly and burst out laughing. Yes, she said, with a tooth missing I really did look frightful. So all right, she'd give me her tooth, as long as I helped her find a friend, because that was the dream she wanted to come true.

She took me by the hand and off we ran.

She said she'd like to take her friend to a meadow and show them a rainbow. She wanted them to smell the scent of wet grass, meet her ma and see where they lived. Then they'd go to the seaside together. There she'd tell her friend about the mystery islands she would sail to one day.

She and her friend would talk and talk forever,
sharing their biggest secrets, dreams and other
very important things.

I loved everything I'd seen. And I thought I'd like to show her something too. So I took her by the hand and we went the other way.

First we went to the park.
There we listened to music
and strolled about in all the
places I love best. Then I
showed her a huge library full
of books I hadn't yet had time
to read. Later we went to
look for butterflies sleeping
among the branches of trees.

After that, it was time for her
to go home.

She said she was pleased to have met me. She wanted to know if we could meet again the next day. I said yes, and promised I'd be right there, waiting for her.

And do you know what else? I gave her back her tooth...

Because I think I'd found what
I was looking for.

First published in the United Kingdom in 2019 by Lantana Publishing Ltd., London.
www.lantanapublishing.com

American edition published in 2019 by Lantana Publishing Ltd., UK.
info@lantanapublishing.com

Original edition published in Polish in 2015 by Nasza Księgarnia, Warsaw, Poland.
This book has been published with the support of the ©POLAND Translation Program.

Text & Illustration © Paweł Pawlak 2019
English translation © Antonia Lloyd-Jones 2019

Distributed in the United States and Canada by Lerner Publishing Group, Inc.
241 First Avenue North, Minneapolis, MN 55401 U.S.A.
For reading levels and more information, look for this title at www.lernerbooks.com
Cataloging-in-Publication Data Available.

Printed and bound in Europe.
Original artwork created as a 3D paper collage and completed digitally.

ISBN: 978-1-911373-79-7
eBook ISBN: 978-1-911373-82-7

OSCAR

has found a friend